THE CRAZY DAY

Louise

Charles

Robert

Sara

William

Fred

First published in Great Britain by HarperCollins*Publishers* in 1999

3 5 7 9 10 8 6 4 2

ISBN: 000 664738-3

From the television series based on
the original Teddybear books
created by Alison Sage and Susanna Gretz.

Text adapted by Alison Sage
Illustrated by Stuart Trotter

Based on an original television series © United Productions
and Link Entertainment. Licensed by Link Licensing
Text and illustrations © Meridian Broadcasting and Link Entertainment

A CIP catalogue record for this title is available from the British Library.

The HarperCollins website address is:
www.**fire**and**water**.com

Printed and bound in Singapore

THE CRAZY DAY

Collins

An Imprint of HarperCollinsPublishers

It was Saturday morning. All the bears had woken up. All, that is, except for Robert. He was fast asleep.

"Get up, lazybones!" said Louise.

"He'll get up when he smells my honey pancakes," said William.

"It's pancakes for breakfast!" cried Sara and Louise, and they rushed downstairs.

"Robert always oversleeps," said Louise.

"I'd hate to miss your pancakes, William," said Charles.

"Mmmm," agreed everyone, with their mouths full.

"Come on, Louise," said Sara after breakfast. "There's lots to do in the garden."

"Yes, *ma'am*," giggled Louise.

"I'm going to read my new book," said Charles.

As they went outside, William looked at the clock.

"I've just got time to get the shopping before lunch," he said.

Upstairs, Robert
rubbed his eyes.
He yawned.
"Where *is*
everyone? Oh, no!
I'm late – and it's pancakes today!"

He scrambled out of bed and
raced downstairs.

He ran into the kitchen.

"Don't eat all the
pancakes!" he cried, but
there was no one there.

Then he looked at the clock. It was a long way past breakfast time.

"It's not fair," he said sadly. "They've eaten them all up, every single one."

All of a sudden, Robert
had an idea.

"I know! If I move the clock hands forwards
to breakfast time, then William will have to
make pancakes again. But the others mustn't
see me doing it!"

He crept up to the clock. Very gently, he
started to move the hands.

Just then, Sara came in from the garden.

"Help!" thought Robert. "She'll see me!"

He dived behind the sofa.

"That Robert!" said Sara. "I bet he's still asleep!" Then she stopped.

The clock said it was time
to take Fred for a walk.

"That's odd!" thought
Sara. "This morning
has gone *very* quickly.
But that clock is never wrong."

She looked round for Fred.
"Come on! Time for
walkies."

Robert crept out from behind the sofa. "Phew! That was close. I'll try again."

Very carefully, he moved the clock hands.

The front door banged and William came in with the shopping.

Again, Robert dived behind the sofa.

"What!" cried William as he saw the clock.
"Lunch time already!" He ran into the kitchen
to start cooking.

Robert peeked
out from behind
the sofa.
"This is harder
than I thought,"
he said. "But I
really want those
pancakes."

He crept up to the clock. He was just
starting to move the hands again when
the garden door opened. It was Charles.

"Oops!" squeaked Robert as he dived
behind the sofa once more.

But Charles was not
looking at Robert.
He was looking at
the clock. His mouth
fell open.

"Tea time!" he cried.
"But I was only reading
under that bush for a few
minutes! I must get to the
library before it shuts."
He rushed out of
the door.

"This is my last try!"
said Robert, pulling at
the hands of the clock.
The garden door banged.

"Not again!" he groaned, diving for the sofa.

This time it was Louise and she was cross.

"No one is helping me. And Robert's still snoring. Anyone'd think it was – BEDTIME!" she cried as she saw the clock. "It's not fair. I *hate* going to bed."

Louise set off up the stairs, still grumbling.

"I think I'd better wait for a bit before I try again," said Robert. He yawned. It was very comfy behind the sofa. Soon he was fast asleep.

Charles walked in with his library book.
He was looking puzzled. Louise came down
the stairs. She looked very puzzled too.
Then Sara arrived with Fred.

"Why did you take Fred for a walk
at bedtime?" said
Louise.

"Bedtime?" said Sara.
"It can't be bedtime."
"But the clock says
it is!" said Louise.
"Hold on," said Charles.
"I think I know what's happening."
"So do I," giggled Louise. "It's–"
Suddenly there was a yell
from the kitchen.
"I've burnt the
lunch!" cried William.
"But it's not
lunch time," said Sara.

William looked at the clock. "Bedtime!"
he cried. "Night, night everyone."
The other bears stared at him.

"It's not bedtime either," laughed Sara.
Louise pointed to the sofa and giggled.
They could all hear the gentle sound
of snoring.

Robert stirred. Then he opened his eyes.

Quickly, the other bears hid behind the door.
Robert tiptoed towards the clock.

"Caught you!" cried Sara and Louise together. "What *are* you up to?"

"I didn't mean to get you all mixed up," said Robert. "I just wanted some pancakes, so I thought I'd make it breakfast time again."

"Is everyone thinking what I'm thinking?" said Charles.

"Yes! Let's all have some more pancakes for lunch," cried William.

And so they did.

Louise

Charles

Robert

William

Sara

Fred

TEDDYBEARS TITLES